EGMONT

We bring stories to life

First published in Great Britain in 2007 by Dean,
an imprint of Egmont UK Limited
239 Kensington High Street, London W8 6SA

Thomas the Tank Engine & Friends™

A BRITT ALLCROFT COMPANY PRODUCTION

Based on The Railway Series by The Reverend W Awdry
Photographs © 2007 Gullane (Thomas) LLC. A HIT Entertainment Company

Thomas the Tank Engine & Friends and Thomas & Friends are trademarks of Gullane (Thomas) Limited.
Thomas the Tank Engine & Friends and Design is Reg. US. Pat. & Tm. Off.

ISBN 978 0 6035 6253 2
1 3 5 7 9 10 8 6 4 2
Printed in Singapore

Harvey to the Rescue

The Thomas TV Series

DEAN

An exciting new engine had arrived on the Island of Sodor. Cranky the Crane unloaded him on to the track.

"He's making my chain ache," groaned Cranky.

When the engine was unloaded, The Fat Controller introduced him. "This is Harvey the Crane Engine," he said, proudly.

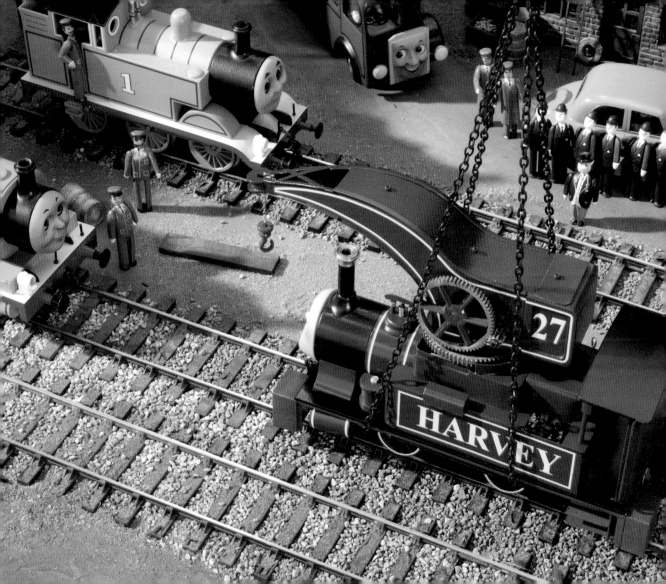

Harvey was happy to be safely on the ground. He didn't like dangling from Cranky's arm at all.

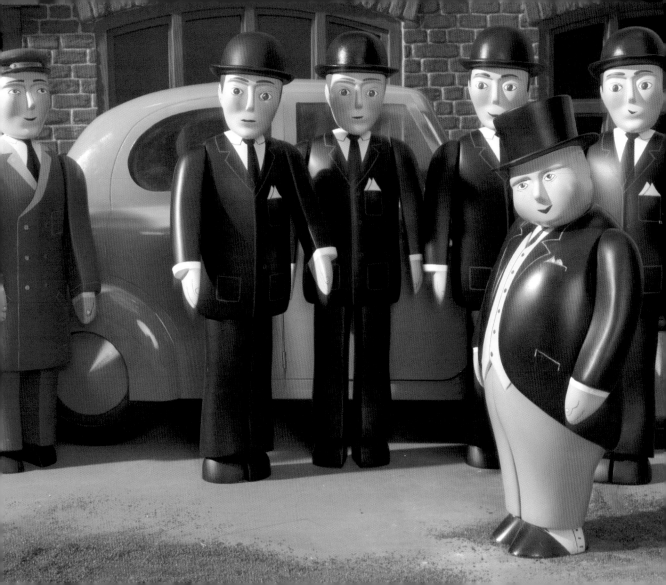

Some gentlemen were standing watching what was going on.

"These are the Gentlemen of the Railway Board," said The Fat Controller. "Tomorrow Harvey will give them a demonstration. If it goes well, he will join the railway."

"What's a 'dimmer station'?" whispered Percy to Thomas.

"Demonstration," said Thomas. "It's when you show off what you can do."

"Like when Thomas and I have a race," said Bertie. "Vrooooomm! Vrooooomm!"

That evening in the engine sheds, Harvey could hear the other engines talking about him.

"Harvey's different," peeped Henry.

"He doesn't even look like an engine," said Edward.

Thomas felt sorry for Harvey. "Don't worry," he whispered to him. "Sometimes it takes time to make new friends!"

But Harvey wasn't sure he wanted to stay where no one wanted him.

The next morning, Harvey said to The Fat Controller, "Maybe I shouldn't have come here, Sir. The engines don't like me. I'm too different."

"Nonsense. Different is what makes you special," The Fat Controller said.

Harvey felt much better after that.

Out on the branch line, Percy was having trouble with the trucks.

"Faster we go, faster we go! Pull him along, don't let him slow!" they chanted.

The trucks went quicker and quicker.

"Heeeeelp!" whistled Percy as the driver pulled on the brakes. But it was too late . . .

CRASH! Percy's front wheels ran off the rails. The trucks shot off down a slope on to the road.

Bertie the Bus had to stop and all the passengers got out to see what had happened.

When The Fat Controller heard about the accident, he went straight to Harvey.

"I was hoping to keep you clean for the demonstration," he said. "But I need you to rescue one of my engines!"

"I'll do my best, Sir," said Harvey, bravely.

In no time at all, Harvey got Percy and the trucks back on the track. The Gentlemen of the Railway Board were very impressed.

"That was the best demonstration of all!" said The Fat Controller. "The Gentlemen have decided you shall join the railway."

"Thank you, Sir," said Harvey, proudly.

That evening in the sheds, Harvey heard the engines talking about him again. But this time their talk was different.

"Isn't Harvey clever!" chuffed Gordon.

"Very useful!" said James.

"You see," said Thomas. "Different can be good!"

All the engines agreed. "Welcome to the Sodor Railway," they called. Harvey smiled happily.